ADOMEE

THE LITTLE BOY
WHO LIVES UNDER THE SEA

G. SCOTT BOLDEN

To order additional copies of this book, contact:
Xlibris
844-714-8691
www.Xlibris.com
Orders@Xlibris.com

ISBN: Softcover   978-1-6698-5912-3
        EBook   978-1-6698-5913-0

Library of Congress Control Number: 2022922770

Print information available on the last page

Rev. date: 12/06/2022

ADOMEE

THE LITTLE BOY
WHO LIVES UNDER THE SEA

Introduction

Deep beneath the beautiful blue sea, a small town flourishes with school, stores and a close knit community. Adomee, a ten year old boy lives with his parents and his younger sister under the sea. His friends call him Adomee. He is a special little boy because he can live under water and on land. He and his friends can swim and walk under the sea and adventure out on land to see the sights of the big city. His adventures on land must be kept a secret to keep his family and friends safe.

Chapter 1

Adomee strolls down the busy bright city street carrying his pail, swinging it back and forth, as he takes in the sights and sounds of the city. The city has tall buildings, a small post office, cute clothing stores, and a fancy-looking library. The honking cars, the children chasing after the ice cream truck, and the dogs chasing squirrels in the park make him smile. The day is warm with clear skies. The weather is warm enough for him to wear his favorite jean shorts and his light blue matching T-shirt. Adomee looks at the blue sky and sees only a few white fluffy clouds. The fluffy clouds look like cotton balls, some small, some medium, and some large. He waves at people passing him on the sidewalk, and he thinks of his mother and his little two-year-old sister, Ana. He thinks Ana is very funny and sweet. He thinks of how she walks and talks and does funny things. Last night Ana went into his room and tried to play with one of his video games. She tried to mimic all of the loud beeping music and sounds that the game made. He also thinks about his mother, Kristina, who was probably at home making dinner for the three of them. His father left this morning to go on a long business trip. His stomach growls as he wonders what his mother is preparing for dinner. He loves pizza, cheeseburgers, and french fries. As he watches an ice cream truck drive away, he wonders if his mother will have one of his favorite ice creams— vanilla, chocolate, or strawberry—for dessert.

As he strolls along the streets, he remembers when he turned ten years old a few months ago, his mother agreed to let him walk downtown by himself. She gave him rules that he promised to follow. He had been sitting on his bed when his mother told him that she was concerned for his safety and that she really didn't want him to go out by himself. He loved the city streets and begged for her to let him go. His father told Adomee's mother that he was ten years of age when he first started going to the city as a young boy, and he believed that Adomee was old enough now to go alone. His mother finally agreed. His mother told him which streets to take and which paths to follow to make sure he would stay safe and would not be followed. She also warned him against mingling with a lot of people on his path.

As he waits on the corner to cross the street to head home, he sees the white sandy beach. He sees the old man, Mr. John, standing at his small wooden stall with a sign that reads "John's Fresh Fish of the Day." Mr. John would fish early in the morning, and then sell the fresh catch of the day to everyone in town. But today, Adomee does not need to buy fish from Mr. John because he has fish in his pail that he caught during the day while fishing with others at the pier.

Adomee looks at the fish in his shiny little pail and counts them, big ones and little ones. He had five little fish and eight big fish. He thinks his mother would be so proud of him. If his father were at home, he would be really proud of him too. His father taught him how to fish.

As he travels along the beach, he sees little children tossing balls on the beach, making sandcastles, filling their buckets with shells, and chasing each other while giggling as they try to catch and tag each other. Maybe he and Ana will play chase this evening when he gets home. He will let her catch him. It is one of their favorite things to do. Ana always claps her hands and giggles as she walks, and after a few minutes, she falls down then gets back up again and starts all over again. He likes to see her run. Ana is too young to come on land. Adomee thinks about the day when they can play in the city, on the beach, together.

As he walks on, he sees the hilly sand dunes with huge birds and remembers what his mother told him. His mother told him, "Do not walk on the sand dunes. They can be dangerous and you could damage the sand and the grass that grows near it." He makes sure that he doesn't go near the sand dunes. As he continues walking, he notices the waves beginning to roll onto the beach. Dark clouds start to roll in. He sees and hears the squall of large and small white birds and sea gulls as they begin to circle above and land on the beach.

Adomee knows that he must walk faster before the weather changes. It will make it harder for him to get home. As he hurries on, he sees many of the adults picking up towels and chairs from the beach where they were sunbathing earlier, playing games, and having fun. They are urging the children to gather up their sand buckets and toys.

Adomee says, "Wow, it's time I go home."

He starts to walk very fast. He is now at the end of the beach where he will soon cross, go down into the water, and swim to his house. He knows his mother can feel the turbulence and is seeing the darkness beginning to settle in. He knows his mother will start to get anxious and worry about him. He does not want his mother and little sister to have to come looking for him. It is now beginning to rain small drops on his head. The weather is no longer warm. It has gotten much cooler, and the fluffy clouds are no longer in the sky. The sky is dark with gray and black clouds. Big drops of rain are falling now. He continues to hurry, and now he can see the stretch of beach where he enters to go into the water.

"Ah," Adomee says as he now enters the darkening sea.

The sea was so beautiful this morning. It was blue, but it is now turning black. Adomee knows that at night, the whole area, the water, and the sky can turn black and become one. As Adomee walks deeper down into the water, he sees the sun shining through the trees, plants, and other vegetation in the water. He is almost home.

He continues to walk and then swims down into the dark sea. He sees a bright white light shining from his home. The deeper Adomee goes down, the closer he gets to the entrance to his home. When Adomee enters his home, his mother smiles.

She says, " I am so glad you made it home in time. I was afraid that Ana and I would have to swim to shore to look for you.". His mom looked at his pail and asked, "What did you bring us?"

He told her he had brought fresh fish that he had caught during the morning. His mother said that she had made pizza and hamburgers, his favorites. She said that tomorrow they would go out to get three flavors of ice cream—vanilla, chocolate, and strawberry. They all looked forward to tomorrow, when they could leave their home, go to the beach, and buy the ice cream.

Chapter 2

AT SCHOOL

It is 7:30 AM. Adomee is at school. He came to school with his mother this morning. His mother is one of the teachers for the Under Water Elementary School (UWE School). Adomee is here before all of the other students and is now waiting for his classmates to arrive. His baby sister, Ana, is at the Under Water Child Care Center. Ana was so happy to see her little friends and teachers when she arrived at the UWCC. She ran to all of them, tripping as she struggled to walk fast, and hugged them.

Adomee now sees his friends arriving in his classroom. Adomee is waiting to see his best friend, Elijah, whom he calls Eli. Eli calls Adomee, Domee. Adomee wants to tell him about his journey yesterday to the town of Vicaris. He wants to tell him all about fishing at the pier, all the people he had seen, and how old man Mr. John was selling fish at his stall outside the pier. Adomee also wants to tell Eli how the children played on the beach until the sky became dark and that their parents told them to gather up all of their belongings and toys because they must head home before the storm comes. He tells him how the water from the sea started rolling in, how the clouds in the sky started to darken, and how it started to rain.

His other classmates are now arriving. They call out his name, saying, "Hi, Domee." Adomee greeted them and told them how he had to walk fast to get home last night before it was too late.

Eli stated that he was almost late last week when he went on land to find the library. Other classmates said that at other times, they also had to rush to get back home when they had stayed out too late looking at all the people, the fun, and the activities on the beach.

At 8:00 AM, Adomee and his friends had to be in their seats in class, so they could no longer talk about their stories about going on land. As school started, the students were taught English, math, social studies, history, world geography, and anatomy of the body (human and sea life anatomy). The students were taught the difference between people who only live on land. They learned how humans breathe by having two organs in their body called lungs and that sea land people also breathe through their skin by taking oxygen from the water.

Adomee and Eli liked school. They learned why the land people could only swim for a little while and not live under water. They now understood why land people could not walk down into the sea and go underwater into their houses to live.

Anatomy fascinated them, as the teacher explained about the breathing system called the respiratory system, and how their lungs and gills extract and use oxygen. The teacher explained their respiratory system and the skin behind their ears pulls the oxygen from the water, while on land, the lungs pull in oxygen.

At lunch time, Adomee and his classmates talked about how much fun it would be to go swimming after school. After lunch, Adomee and his classmates went back to their classroom, where he passed his mother in the hallway. She had just finished her lunch with the teachers. Adomee and his mother smiled and greeted each other. Adomee had just a few more hours, and then he could go swimming. Time went by too slowly for Adomee, but now it is time for the swim period. All of the children were so excited. They have thirty minutes to swim, and then the bell will ring for them to get out of the water, get dressed, and get back to class.

While in the sea, the children played in the warm water. The sky was so blue with not a cloud in sight. The children swam with dolphins and large and small fish. They fish were of many colors—red, gold, blue, multiple colors, and some almost transparent. Adomee had seen some of the fish sleeping against rocks in the ocean last night. The swim bell rang. It is now time to go back to class.

In their next period, they were given an assignment to visit the library the next day and check out books they would like to read. They were told to be careful with the books, take good care of them, and not to lose them. Adomee and the children were told that there were many books at the Aspire Sea Bright Library on Resort Beach. Each child was given a library card to check out four books assigned by the teacher and any other books they wanted to read. The teacher also gave them a special bag for the books so the books would not get wet when the students went under water to return home.

Tomorrow would be a great day. They talked about the books they were going to get from the library. Adomee said he was going to get one or two books for little kids, and he would read them to Ana. He said he would also get a nice book for his mother to read. Eli said he was going to get a book on cars and toys and also a scary book.

Chapter 3

AT THE LIBRARY

The next day, Adomee and ten of his friends set out to visit the library. There were six girls, Poppy, Cassie, Rita, Tristan, Violet, and Journey. The four boys were Elijah, Samuel, Thomas, and Ralphie.

The library sits on the corner of Sea Short Road and Beach Street.

"wow!" they all say, "look at that building."

What a large building it is. It is painted blue and pink with orange fish designs. The building has many, many windows with green trees and flowers of various colors—yellow, red, purple, and pink. Some of the flowers are roses, geraniums, and irises. The library was so pretty. Land people of all ages are going into the library, and some people are coming out with books in their arms. Eli and his friends take their time entering the revolving door to stand in the beautiful, quiet lobby of the library.

Eli says, "I hope they did not take the books I wanted."

As all the children take in the sights of this enormous room with rows and rows of books, they hope that the land people haven't taken the books that they wanted to take home. They are so excited. They had never seen so many books. They saw all kinds of books—colorful books with small and large words, comic books, scary-looking books, and school books on all kinds of topics, such as anatomy and history. Some books were about science, religion, mystery, and children tales. They saw many books on foods, such as meats, vegetables, fruits, desserts, and beverages. They all started to talk at once about the books. They were so happy that smiles filled their faces. The librarian told them to remember the rules, not to talk too loud, and that they were to remain quiet while in the library so they would not disturb other people.

After an hour of trying to decide which books they wanted to take home, the librarian helped each of the children get the books they wanted to check out. Each of the children checked out seven to eight books.

The librarian told them when they brought them back that they could get more books. She also told them to bring more of their friends next time to get some books or attend a story reading class. The children were so happy. They put their books in their special book bags. As they headed home, they were laughing, skipping, and singing songs.

Once at home, the children told their parents about their day. Adomee gave his mother the two books he had brought for her to read. The books he brought to read to Ana had dinosaurs, the sun and moon, and people walking dogs. One of the books for Ana played music when opened. Ana loved the books. She laughed and made noises as she pointed to the characters in the book. Ana pretended to read first one book, then the other book.

Soon it was time to get ready for bed. The night was approaching, and it was time for Adomee to get ready for another day. What a wonderful, fun day it had been. Tomorrow would be another wonderful day. Tomorrow would be the day when their school's Olympic sports games would be held. There would be swim races, water activities, jumping rope, and sports, such as baseball.

Chapter 4

A DAY OF EXERCISE

Today is the big day of water sports. After morning classes, Adomee and his classmates went to lunch. They were so excited that they could barely eat their lunches. They ate sandwiches, chips, and fruits, and they drank fruit juices. They had ice cream for dessert. After lunch, they went back to class to learn more about water paths, water sports, and water safety. They learned about limitations while in the water, how far they could go, and how deep they could travel in the water. They were told that it was best to swim in the afternoon when the water has warmed up.

Later in the afternoon, the teachers took Adomee and his classmates out into the sea. They all loved the water. Adomee and Eli seemed to be the best swimmers, and they were able to help their classmates as they practiced strengthening their legs, concentrating on how to swim for long periods of time by using their skin and gills. They practiced where and how to enter the sea and where and how to exit the water.

Adomee thought of his baby sister, Ana, who was now being kept by the babysitter. The babysitter would give Ana a short class today on water exercise. As Ana gets older, she will continue to get water exercise lessons until she is able to be a strong swimmer like Adomee.

The water classes were fun. Everyone swam and walked in the water until it was time to go home. What a wonderful day. Now it is time to go home, rest, and have dinner. Adomee told his mother and Ana about the water classes, about how much he loved the classes, and about how he really enjoyed being with his friends. He stated that he was looking forward to the next water sports day. Adomee showed Ana how he moved in the water, moving his arms and his legs. Ana tried to imitate her big brother as she moved her little arms and legs and giggled. Soon she fell asleep.

The next day, Adomee and his mother took Ana to the sea with them to teach her how to swim. They did not take Ana out very far in the water. It was going to be a fun day, playing in the water with her mother and her brother. After a day filled with fun, Adomee, Ana, and their mother went home. Mother prepared pizza and ice cream. They loved this meal.

It soon started getting dark. Ana stated she wanted to play with her toys and dolls before going to bed. While playing with her dolls, Ana fell asleep. She had a busy day. She loved trying to swim as Adomee and her mother showed her how to move her arms and legs. Later she enjoyed eating her favorite foods and playing with her toys and dolls. Now she was fast asleep.

Tomorrow would be another day. Adomee, Ana, and their mother, along with his classmates and teachers, would start all over again. Another week of school, where they will learn and explore new things.